GIVE ME THE MOUNTAINS

For my family and friends

Crumps Barn Studio
Syde, Cheltenham GL53 9PN
www.crumpsbarnstudio.co.uk

Text copyright © Anne Swan 2025

The right of Anne Swan to be identified as the author of this work has been asserted in accordance with the Copyright, Designs and Patents Act 1988.

The author wishes to state that this is a fictionalised memoir and all characters and situations mentioned are her creation, except where references are made to public figures or events already in the public record. Any similarity to persons living or dead is entirely coincidental.

All rights reserved. No part of this publication may be reproduced, stored in a retrieval system, or transmitted in any form or by any means, electronic, mechanical, photocopying, recording or otherwise, without the prior permission of the copyright owner.

Cover design by Lorna Gray

Typeset in Adobe Garamond Pro

All our books are printed on responsibly sourced paper from a mixture of managed woodlands and recycled material. Printed in the UK by CMP, Poole.

ISBN 978-1-915067-60-9

GIVE ME THE MOUNTAINS

Anne Swan

Crumps Barn Studio

A NOTE FROM THE AUTHOR

This is a fictionalised memoir. Although this book has been inspired by real historical events, the author wishes to state that the people, dialogue and interactions within these pages are her creation. No comparison is intended with the friends and family members from her past or present life.

CELIA

They had fallen in love and knew they wanted to marry. So he must call upon her parents and say he wished to have their permission to ask for Celia's hand in marriage. They were both English but living in New York, he because of his work, she because of her father's work. Her parents lived at the top of a block of flats overlooking Central Park. It had one of those lifts that only stops at their condominium – or maybe it was a penthouse; but evidently 'there was money'.

Her mother was clearly not pleased, neither with the young man proposing to be her son-in-law nor with the idea of her daughter getting married at all; she found it useful to have her around and act as an unpaid maid. In fact, Celia had arrived thirteen years after the other four children, she was not wanted and had been told so at a young age. Apparently the doctor had said to her mother 'Never mind, she can be a comfort in your old age'. Celia felt she was given everything she could ever want as long as she stayed; expensive clothes, jewellery, onyx ashtray and matching lighter, two dogs, a small roadster etc. And once a week a singing lesson; she had a good contralto voice and it was an accomplishment to be encouraged. But, having been asked to join the Carl Rosa Opera Company, her mother immediately said no. "No daughter of mine is going on the stage."

Before going to America the family had lived in England. Celia had two sisters and two brothers; one was badly wounded in the First World War in the army, and was in a field hospital in France. Her mother was not taking no for an answer and managed to get over to France and see her son before he died. When the war ended, once a year she and another daughter would collect a wreath, take the train, the ferry and then the French train to Etaples; lay the wreath and then make the journey back home. They would sit on the ferry on deckchairs tied to the rails, clutching paper bags (provided by the ferry), in case they felt or were seasick.

Her second son had served in the navy. He had been married, but divorced; so had to leave the Service. But he was recalled when the Second World War started – and drowned while swimming to the rescue of a pilot who had been shot down near the ship. Being a good swimmer, he had dived in but when the plane sank he was sucked down with it. Her mother wore black for at least a year, together with his medals. Then for the rest of her life, she wore purple; and the dining room carpet was dyed purple too. She had lost both her sons in the wars.

In England they lived in the country; there was a lake in the grounds and two cormorants were purchased – from Harrods? It used to be said that you could buy anything from Harrods, from a coat to a crocodile. These birds were expected to catch the fish in the lake for the household to eat, presumably using the Chinese way of tying a string round the bird's neck so, having caught a fish, the cormorant couldn't eat it. One had died, thank goodness from Celia's point of view as she was expected to take the other out in a rowing boat so it could do its fishing. She hated the cormorant and while rowing the boat it would attack her, pecking her bare legs until they were sore. She was about twelve. The family say they were geese, not cormorants; but you wouldn't take a goose fishing.

In 1917 her parents moved permanently to America, so Celia went to boarding school in England. She would stay at the school during the school holidays. But the long summer holiday allowed her mother to take the ship from New York, see her for some weeks, buy any new clothes needed – and oversee Celia doing any necessary mending. Celia was left-handed, but made to write with her right hand. She loved games, but wasn't allowed to play tennis or golf as it was considered impossible for left-handers. She sailed to America to join her parents on holiday in 1919; would she like to go to school in New York and stay with them? She declined, and went back to London. When she finally left school she went to join them.

But Celia's had been a rather lonely, strange childhood. Only towards the end of her schooling did she go somewhere she thoroughly enjoyed, where she met and made lifelong friends, going to stay with them during the school holidays.

Celia had met her suitor in New York at a New Year's Eve party – her father, who worked for a big UK company, had invited him saying he couldn't be on his own as a British person, so he must join the family. He did, and the two young obviously clicked.

If any man showed an interest in Celia, her mother would arrange for her to be taken abroad by married friends from her husband's company to act as a companion for their wives. So, realizing a potential suitor was here, Celia was packed off with a couple going to Florida. But this time the plan did not work as the wife was a friend of Celia's and she realized that the mother was doing this to keep the two apart. So Celia went to Florida with the couple who then went off leaving her in the hotel. A few days later Celia's future husband came to Florida, staying in his usual hotel; he went there each year in order to keep in touch with his clientele. So the two had a wonderful time, staying in separate hotels, and falling in love totally. He proposed and she accepted; two and a half months after they first met. But there were two conditions; as a bachelor he'd enjoyed gambling (not very successfully, as I understand) – that had to stop! And he must agree to her having her two dogs!

So arrangements were made for Celia's fiancé to call on her parents and formally request their permission to marry her. Her father was a dear – a kind man; but henpecked. The interview did not go well and her mother said firmly that they could see each other once a week for a year and then, if they still felt the same way they could discuss marriage. This was a blow, but her fiancé felt that, out of respect, he must accept their decision. So he gave a little bow to them both and went to the lift to leave. Her father accompanied him and, as he opened the lift door, he said quietly, "Take no notice. Go ahead and get married."

They made their plans to marry at a registry office (in Wall

Street) as soon as possible. No one was to know. Two cleaners would be witnesses. She could take very few belongings with her as she did not want her mother to suspect anything. When the big day came, she said she was going to a singing lesson, and left. Her music case did not contain music. After they were married she rang home and told her mother who said you'd better come tomorrow and collect your things; anything you do not take, will no longer be yours. And the phone was put down. Her husband rang to speak to his new father-in-law who said he wished them well; and that Celia should come and collect what she wanted when her mother was not around.

As they were now living in a small bachelor flat, there was very little room for furniture, so she only managed to collect a few small items. But Celia's father met up with her husband once a week from then on, without telling her mother, and they became good friends. This was the start of a long and happy marriage. There were three children.

Celia was left a set of dentures, in her mother's Will. Apparently these can sometimes have some value.

Give Me the Mountains

Give me the mountains, those great craggy peaks
Where the air is brilliant and the silence speaks.
Great jagged rocks whose jaws slash the sky
Like fangs that snap at clouds scudding by.

Give me the sharpness of age-harrowed rock.
The harshness of granite that dares to mock
The valley below lying soft and green.
Give me the mountains where no man has been.

Oh mountains, oh air, oh power and might!
What glorious strength – what beauty, what height.
You challenge our courage, with danger and dread,
And yet – oh! what glory for those who dare tread
Your desolate places; your grim and grey stone.

There Man is with God and himself, and alone.

Down Dragonfly Lane

Often I cycle down Dragonfly Lane
And yesterday I did so again –
The over-ripe blackberries trembled and fell;
The air was thick with their too-sweet smell …
An autumn-come/summer-gone scent
From berries now scattered and squashed as I went
Along.

As always I saw and heard
The pigeons, jackdaws – the smaller bird
Such as linnet, goldfinch, warbler too.
While starlings this year are very few …

(No murmurations here …
They spread disease, some farmers fear.)

Tardy house martins and swallows took flight
On their mega migration … a half-happy sight.
They know when the time has come to leave;
And, while glad to see them, we also grieve
For summer is over – and departures are sad.

There were fewer swifts than we usually had.

But autumn brings special joys for I see
The dragonflies that accompany me
As I cycle. They'd fly ahead, beside, behind;
Settle on brambles, the bushes that lined
The lane. Dragonfly jewels, with bodies that gleam,
Sparkle and glisten in the sun ... they seem
Like little enamelled dragons, whence springs
A double set of incredible wings.

The Emperor is biggest, a sapphire blue,
While the small red and green demoiselles too
Fly alongside keeping pace with me –
Acting as my escorts! Sometimes there'd be
The banded damselfly – velvety green,
Darkly beautiful. Such lovely things seen.

COURT CIRCULAR

She thought she'd faint. She could feel herself going numb, so she clutched the back of the seat in front of her, willing herself to stay upright … not to collapse till she had got off the bus and into her flat. It couldn't be true; it just Could Not Be True. But it was: there in black and white in a Court Circular in a national newspaper. She must be careful because of their child. *Their* child?! No! Not *theirs*! Not *their* anything. Any more. Ever. Only *her* child now, for she was seven months pregnant and had just seen the announcement saying the man she loved, lived with and was the father of her child, had been married in Paris.

She wouldn't think about it, wouldn't allow herself to until she had got home, had shut the door and was alone. Then she could allow herself to think, to try to take in the utterly devastating fact that she would be alone. No, not would be, but WAS on her own. And he hadn't even told her. Not a word, not a sign; no communication at all. He had just stepped out of her life. But for the baby's sake, she must remain calm. It became her mantra.

Everything was a blur and she never remembered the rest of the journey home. Later she wanted to scream, to scream until she could scream no more. But she must not, would not because of her baby. At times she did begin to shake, uncontrollably. It was unutterably awful, unbearable, beyond belief. It was beyond her. How would she cope? There was so much she'd have to think out, plan for, arrange etc. She'd have to move, have to get more work, have to find a childminder, have to find out where to have a baby – all without *her man* at her side to help and support. Would he help financially? Or not? Would her parents? But then, would she tell them? They knew nothing of her pregnancy; they lived up north and were happy that she was doing well in London and had a 'nice boyfriend'. What would she tell them? What would she tell anyone? Would she, in fact, tell anyone?

But how come she'd failed to notice that he no longer loved her? They'd both been at university where they'd met, enjoyed each other's company for some years and then started living together. They'd been together for two years now. She was so happy to be with him and when pregnant had no concerns as she'd sort of assumed they would marry and live happily ever after. Yes. She'd assumed: but evidently he had not. But he hadn't told her.

Looking back she realised he had started to go away for long weekends without her; saying it was to meet the right people and get commissions (he was an architect) and he couldn't take her as it was business and, anyway, being so obviously pregnant she couldn't go too. Although this was 1935, when so many things were changing, customs, morals, women having careers, running their own lives, she hadn't expected to accompany him, particularly when very clearly pregnant. No, she had suspected nothing. What a fool. She wept, or would have wept except there were no tears left. She was utterly devastated. But she must try not to get too upset, for her baby's sake.

The Court Circular simply stated that by special licence the Hon. P had married Mr X at the British Embassy in Paris. November 1935. Where had they met? When? For how long had they been going out together? Why Special Licence? Did that mean they'd had to get married? Had he got her pregnant – and being a posh family they couldn't have a child born out of wedlock? Or was he madly in love with her – along with a bit of social climbing? Everyone did that; they all wanted to better themselves, get on in life. Unbelievably, this new wife of his (how that word hurt) had the same first name as she did. So no worries there about calling your lover by the wrong name, she thought bitterly.

But practicalities were needed now, for herself and child. So she enrolled in a secretarial college in order to earn more money and have regular work. She did languages at university, so could teach as well. She made all the arrangements she could to ensure her baby came into a world with a mother able to love and look after her. Having decided she must tell her parents, she did eventually ring and spoke to her mother; but it somehow proved impossible to broach the subject. Her mother had kept wittering on about banalities, such as some flowers which had been sent to her, how they were almost dead and an absolute disgrace and whether she should tell the people who sent them or the flower shop, or both! etc. etc. (they were sweet peas). In the end she just gave up and, in fact, she never did tell them; nor her sisters.

She moved to a town near London, near an address where unmarried mothers could go, and after giving birth to a daughter the two of them began their new life together – à deux, not à trois as she had always assumed would be the case.

When it came to registering the birth, she contacted the father saying she wished to pop in and see him. However, he said she couldn't do that but must make an appointment. She didn't quite understand why, but made the appointment – in her lunch hour, as she was working. On arrival she found two other men there so she said this was a personal matter that she had to discuss with him. But he replied that one man was his brother, the other his solicitor and she should say what she had to say in front of them all.

At this, she said she had come to ask if he wanted his name to appear on his daughter's birth certificate – but in view of what he had just said, she would not wish her daughter to be burdened with his name. And left. Now she knew why he would not see her on her own!

For a year and half she worked all she could and paid for a childminder; but eventually the work and stress took its toll and she became ill and was hospitalised for some days. When she recovered, she went to collect her daughter, only to find that the childminder had handed her over to the workhouse[*] because she had not been paid. The worry and stress of it all eventually caused another collapse, which happened in a high street by a telephone box and an elderly couple she

---

[*] The last workhouses closed in 1948

knew saw her, took her home and insisted on being told what was going on. So the whole story came out; it was the first time she had told anyone.

She clearly could not go on trying to do so much on her own, as it was making her ill; the couple felt it would be best to have her daughter adopted, giving her a more secure home and better start to life. A heartbreaking decision to make; but this was eventually agreed and the couple helped by making all the arrangements and providing the required layette and so on.

They were incredibly kind, and constant in their friendship.

Years later she did marry and had another daughter. She died in her eighties. She never knew that her second daughter traced the half-sister and that they became good friends.

The Pool

A little stream runs down to a pool
Where the trees keep it sheltered, shady and cool.
Kingfishers come and search here for fish
Perching quite near; no one could wish
For a lovelier place.

Then people arrive to lark
Around in the water, with their dogs that bark,
Chase sticks and balls; while the kids splash about,
Enjoying themselves as they laugh and shout.

So Nature retires, withdraws from the scene.
No one would guess what creatures had been
Here earlier. The feathered, the furred – now gone
        from sight,
Disappearing until the time is right
For them to return – that's when noises cease,
People depart, and the pool is at peace
Again. Then Nature reclaims her world.

I, Unthinking

And I, unthinking, had such fun – was surely not the
        only one –
As selfishly I drove my car down country lanes, both near
        and far,
While noxious fumes spread everywhere polluting once
        pure atmosphere.

I've flown in planes to distant lands – o'er mountain peaks
        and desert sands;
Rivers, forests, jungles too as I, unthinking, chose to do.
Took my pleasure without care; selfishly I did my share
Of burning oil and coal and gas, greatly adding to the mass
Of toxic plastic, litter and – (now, too late,) I understand
Just what hurt, what harm we've done. We trashed this
        planet having fun.

Rare earths, minerals, water too … all extracted so
        Man can do
Clever things with them and have light and heat, tv, satnav.
Smart phones, fridges, gadgets galore … whatever we have,
        we still want more.

Now fish can't breathe in toxic seas; and noxious sprays
    afflict our bees,
Insects, birds and other small creatures; many, if not all,
Will die. See a *pest* and what do we do? Powder, pellet,
    spray it to
Extinction. We never fail to kill the slug,
    the beautiful snail –
That food so important to the thrush who, come the dawn
    and evening's hush,
Sings for us his treetop song, a sound to enchant us
    and astound.
Heart-stopping to think that such a bird could silent be,
    his voice unheard.

Yes – I, unthinking, share the blame. And, thinking now,
    hang head in shame.

EARLY YEARS AND THE WAR

Old Fozzy was a gardener. He was The Gardener. They lived in Essex, now part of Greater London, but then quite rural. The house was on a slope, with a bit of land behind it, and flower beds and two lawns in front. Then the high street. Old Fozzy was one of her earliest memories. His boots were old, and worn, but clearly comfy; he had bits of string tied round his trousers below the knee, whether to keep the bottoms of his trousers clean or to prevent insects from climbing up wasn't clear. Perhaps for both reasons. His hands were like the bark of an old oak tree and surprisingly gentle. He could remove a small unwanted weed without disturbing neighbouring plants and he could move insects, in danger of being trodden on or swept away, to a safer place without alarming them.

Old Fozzy wore an apron – canvas? hessian? – with a big pocket for useful things like a penknife, string, raffia and pruning knife. A weskit, a pocket there overflowing with a large coloured kerchief. His hair was once dark but now a mixture of greys, captured under a cloth cap. His moustache was splendid and resembled a broom for sweeping the yard; grey with brown stains from the tobacco he smoked in a pipe. He smelled of tobacco. You knew when he was around.

There had been a great excitement during the war; there were bombs and doodlebugs and shrapnel to collect. Doodlebugs were nasty as you could hear their engines and when it cut out and there was silence you knew the bomb would come down. Air raid sirens wailing – it was an upsetting time. The cat had to be put down; it was so frightened. Once she found a bomb, about a foot long with a propellor thing one end; it was in the laurels near the road. When she showed it to the family the police were called, who removed it. When he heard about this, Old Fozzy said he'd found it on the lawn some days previously and had chucked it into the shrubbery!

Apparently, old ammo had been checked for safety and then transported by truck through the town; someone had tossed bombs over the fences into people's gardens – for fun – as they drove by.

The country was asked to grow more food so Old Fozzy dug up the lawn to make a vegetable garden and he grew cabbages and carrots and parsnips and potatoes there. And then they needed a proper air raid shelter, so one was built at the back of the house. There was a Morrison shelter in the sitting room by the kitchen where the nanny/cook lived. This was a large metal thing like a table, and she and her brother slept under it – all snugged up and feeling safe. They used the top as a table and played board games on it … using farthings as counters, those little coins with wrens on them; they kept lots in a green felt bag. They were lovely.

The new air raid shelter had four bunks in it, two on one side, two on the other, with all the feet meeting in one corner. Hers was the bottom bunk. Having said she wanted to be on the top bunk, she had to be rescued, screaming and brought down to her own – she was too terrified on the top one. The illusion of safety.

One morning on arriving at the nursery school at the other end of the town they found the school wasn't there; it was just rubble with smoke rising from what was left. Then their parents decided the children should be evacuated to the country and arranged for them to live with some other children in a big country house in Rutland.

Everyone had gas masks which they carried in a square cardboard box on a string slung over one shoulder. Masks for children were made to look like Mickey Mouse, so they were like a toy and not at all frightening. She must have seen the black and white newsreels in the cinema because, years later when reminiscing with her brother, she said how she remembered being on the station waiting to go by train, everyone with their gas mask and a label on the lapel of their coat. Her brother said that was total rubbish. Father had driven them up to Rutland to see for himself where they would be and meet the family who lived in the house. Children were indeed being evacuated as the government required; thousands went by train. But this was a private arrangement, three or four other children – and a Mademoiselle to teach them reading and writing and maths etc. So much for memory! She'd obviously seen the newsreels. Other memories, many years later, were also found to be inaccurate in that it was a surprise to see the roof tiles were red; she hadn't remembered any colour … so must be remembering black and white photos.

But what a wonderful place to live and grow up in! For ever after, the countryside was the love of their lives. There was a lake in front of the house; terraces and flowerbeds, then lawns and then fields and the lake. Farmland all round and there were cows with horns, carthorses pulling carts, a tractor – probably a Fordson; orange, and they could sit on the mudguards over the wheels; it went faster if you pulled the metal thing with teeth further out and hooked it down. They got scratched to bits by the stubble when the grain was being harvested. They stooked stooks, and when there was only a little patch remaining to be cut, she'd go out early and shout and try to get the rabbits to run off and get away safely.

Hay was cut and piled into large heaps – large to them, probably not so huge in reality. But a thick rope was put on the ground round a heap and attached to a cart horse who then walked, slowly dragging the hay to the barn nearby. A wagon, a proper haywain, blue with bits of red paint at the ends, was pulled by the carthorse. Hay had been tossed up to the man there, pitchforked from the ground. She, ever wanting to show off, insisted on driving the horse and cart out of the field and up to the yard. Overconfident, she decided to stand up as she held those wonderful long leather, studded reins going over the saddle, through the hames, and on to the horse. Misjudging the gateway, she managed to hit the righthand post, and then fell down through the horse's tail and on to the ground amongst his huge hooves and fabulous feathers. That memory is still as clear as ever; the large, shiny rump and tail – and the hooves. But the horse avoided hurting her and she was unscathed. Horses always avoid hurting you if they can.

A Land Girl working there had a boyfriend in the Air Force and he'd fly over and waggle his wings at her and them. It was difficult trying to teach them anything. Everyone spent their time gazing out of the window; and her brother used to daydream, swinging his legs and kicking Mademoiselle black and blue.

Some evacuees were so happy in the country, they didn't want to leave it. Which was hard for their parents. Down Plymouth way, at the end of the working day whole families removed to the countryside nearby, in order to escape the nightly bombing raids. There was the blackout, so lights were not allowed and signposts were removed or covered; car drivers had to mask their headlights, it was not easy moving around. Of course there was less traffic; a friend who drove the Americans preparing for Operation Overlord said it was very tricky as she didn't know the area and had virtually no signposts or lights. She never spoke of her work until she was nearly eighty; and neither did another friend who'd been at Bletchley.

Bathtime was three or four in the bath; turns taken to 'drive' the bath, being in front and pulling the plug on the chain. There was a cork-topped stool by the bath and they were jumped out and into a big towel on the lap of whoever was in charge. Religious tales and poems – *The Arab's Farewell to his Steed*, she loved that one – were recited to them; but nothing frightening like *Struwwelpeter* and *Alice in Wonderland*. Both horrid, with horrid pictures.

One time, the tooth fairy visited her when she had a tooth

come out and put it under her pillow. In the morning there were tiny footsteps in silver gossamer from the door to her bed … what an impression that made on her! Looking back, they must have scattered a path of Lux soap flakes and then made tiny footsteps with a doll; it was a lovely thing to do.

She was taken ill and had to go to hospital for some weeks. Caused by eating artificial cream, they said. Paratyphoid. She couldn't walk as she was so weak, but when she eventually got going she put her slippers on – and found earwigs had nested in one. It was heaving. The hospital consisted of wooden sheds. Matron kept chickens behind one, and had a hen with a clutch of eggs. But the mother hen kept pushing one egg out. So Matron brought it in to her to try to hatch; she was to hold it on her lap in bed. It didn't hatch, so the hen was right. But she didn't enjoy having the egg, being afraid it might break.

When she came to leave the hospital, Matron said she was looking so pale that they would have to put her in the hospital ovens to brown her a bit before she left; so she was scared when the time came – and hugely relieved when she wasn't put in an oven. Her father collected her in his car and drove her home. Her next home would be at a prep school in the country.

They'd hear scraps of stories to do with the war, many of which made little sense till years later. There was a nice military man who was widowed; but his wife had taken to drink, which had eventually killed her. She had gone into the air raid shelter after a raid and found everyone dead. There wasn't a mark on any of them; the blast had killed them all, including her children.

There were two brothers back from the war, one of whom had been in Burma; he was emaciated with sparse white hair, although only in his forties. He could have been his brother's grandfather. They were told not to stare at him.

When learning to type years later there was a teacher who was vast, clearly glandular – as used to be said then. It must have been so hard to cope with all those stones of unwanted weight. She knitted all her clothes, enormous skirts in dark wool etc. She couldn't have bought anything her size. Later we learned that, aged twelve, she'd been in bed one night when there was a raid and the house was hit. She was trapped for over twenty-four hours – unable to move or free herself. A terrifying ordeal. When she was rescued she kept saying she was hungry.

Apparently, fire brigades in rural areas would go to London at weekends to give the London firefighters a rest; not a thing she'd ever thought of, but it was clearly necessary and must have been a great help. And a worry for those leaving 'safe' areas.

At school they knew nothing of the celebrations at the end of the war; with the scenes outside Buckingham Palace. Described on the wireless, no doubt, and in the newspapers – and Illustrated London News etc. But they were told the war had ended, it was over and they were glad.

Churchill sent a printed message to all children saying, *"Today as we celebrate Victory I send this personal message to you and all boys and girls ..."* and the rest has been forgotten – and the original lost.

Why Willows Weep

Now I know why willows weep …
For hereabouts they may not keep
Their golden tresses, which they trail
Over the brook. They never fail
To please, enchant us and delight:
'Twas always such a lovely sight.

The willow, the water, a peaceful scene
Where generations of children have been
Introduced to nature's joys – wide eyed,
Thrilled by all they caught sight of and tried
To identify, to correctly name.
Where they'd play the Poohsticks game.

Yes, many the people who paused and stayed
To watch the water as it played
With the willow's fronds, then rippled on:
Today that lovely scene has gone.
 Now just a memory, though for some like me,
That willow was never a nuisance tree.

The Dark Bush Cricket

Suddenly, to my surprise,
I realised a pair of eyes
Were fixed unblinkingly on me ...

There, in the shed I could see
A little cricket on the mower.
I made my movements slower,
Propped the shed door open wide
Then quietly made my way inside.

(He – a male because he had no thing
At the end of his body, like a sting ...
The ladies have that, behind their legs –
An ovipositor for laying eggs ...)

Anyway, his legs were large, angular, strong –
His antennae too incredibly long;
His colour – pale brown, with a line near his eye ...
Unless he was moving you'd pass him by.

I picked up the cloth he was sitting on,
Expecting him to jump and be gone –
But he didn't move; so I carried him out
And waited while he looked about ...

Then slowly walked off into the grass.

He didn't seem worried and I watched him pass
From our world back to his own ... I could see him alright –
Then not at all! he'd simply gone, vanished from sight.
What a treat when we're trusted by the creatures we meet.

Afterthought

I'm very glad that they're really small –
If they were large they'd scare us all witless!

FINISHED OFF

After the war, the country got back to the Season when young ladies were on show like the racehorses in the paddock prior to a race. You were very desirable as a wife, and the young men going to the dances – and balls – were naturally eminently suitable as husbands; one or both sexes being titled and probably landed, with estates in the country as well as a town house. It was all very splendid and the right people mixed with the other right people. In most cases their parents would all have known each other since birth.

For those aspiring to be Presented at Court, and to Come Out, finishing schools were a must – particularly if you had neither title nor land. Money, of course, was always very welcome; a huge help. There was the Queen Charlotte's Ball, known colloquially as … without the C. But that disappeared, as did going to curtsey in front of Her Majesty. But coming out was still something to be desired and was now achieved by 'doing' the London Season. As a young lady coming out, you were making your debut in Society and were known as a debutante. The young men who were your escorts were known as debs' delights. Most mothers and grandmothers of the debs would have been presented in their time at court and curtsied before the Monarch.

Mothers were very keen for this to be the culmination of years of (an expensive) education; it would 'open doors'. Whatever the cost, doing the Season would be a wonderful experience … and who knows, a daughter might meet—? who knows who?! So finishing schools became very important as they equipped young ladies with the skills needed to run a stately home. There were also some well-connected, maybe titled but not wealthy, ladies who for considerable sums of money would undertake to steer someone's daughter through the season, thus enabling her to meet, mingle, mix with, and possibly marry an eligible bachelor. This would be to the satisfaction of all concerned.

There were several finishing schools in London, one being near South Kensington where French would be studied, as well as etiquette, posture, and some needlework, some cookery. Each week there would be a visit to a social event – part of the season. At the end of that term, they would all go to the ball – the young ladies wearing white – held at the Dorchester. Tennis would be practised at Queen's Club for those interested in a little gentle sport. It was all very ladylike. Under *posture*, one was taught how to enter a room, never by turning your back to the room while you shut the door, and then facing the room.

No, one should come in, facing and smiling at the people there, swing the door shut behind one – and shut it while looking pleasantly at the people watching one's entry. It can be tricky, for doorknobs or handles all require different handling – and care should be taken not to shut one's skirt in the door inadvertently. This can be embarrassing as one steps forward, hand outstretched to meet people – always with an attractive smile of greeting – only to get halted abruptly. This then means having to back up to the door to try and open it behind one, and rescue the garment; consequently the whole effect is ruined. So careful practice is needed.

They dined, taking it in turns to sit next to the Head – practising polite conversation and filling awkward gaps with genteel remarks. Someone must have taken chewing gum out of their mouth and stuck it under the table. Another girl felt it and said, "Oh, look what I've found!" Shock horror! One should carry on chatting charmingly; not bat an eyelid, just ignore it.

Most of the ladies enrolled there were suitable, being interested in boys, painting their nails, doing their hair and comparing clothes and fashion. One tall, strapping lass – Lydia – came from Kenya; she had not been vetted prior to arrival – and would probably not have been welcomed to the establishment had this happened. She had a loud, uninhibited laugh – and if she thought something ridiculous she would say so, loudly. She was fun and had been used to riding horses every day as well as being outdoors all and every day. Her time in London did not prove very enjoyable.

The brochure was splendid showing visits, always accompanied by Mam'zelle of course, to Ascot, Wimbledon, Chelsea Flower Show, Henley Royal Regatta, the Derby. The ladies did indeed go to them – by coach, and were then left to their own devices till the coach took them home. This happened at every event. Our heroines didn't actually set eyes on a horse at Ascot. They had no seats at Wimbledon, so had strawberries and cream instead of tennis. At the Chelsea Flower Show Mam'zelle was with them until they managed to lose her behind the cacti plants. They then went off to buy ice cream. At Henley it was impossible to get near the river, so some went for a walk in the town. At the Derby many opted for the pleasures of the fairground wooden roundabout horses and much enjoyed riding them. A cultural experience indeed.

There was the odd visit to the National Gallery and The Tate … always with Mam'zelle, which was an inhibiting factor for those who would have preferred to chat up the boys there on school trips; far more interesting than pictures. Though there was one startling occasion when they found themselves in front of a large painting of a nude lady, in a reclining position – this caused acute embarrassment, a sudden silence … and a rapid retreat to another room full of wonderful oil paintings of Highland cattle.

The highlight of the Season, the Ball, finally took place; the ladies having first been introduced to the male escorts who had arrived to take them to the Dorchester in chauffeur driven Bentleys etc. Having been formally introduced to the Duke of This and the Earl of That, the ladies were informed that they could now go out with said young titles, should they be asked. A few of the young ladies would be coming out that season. Their mothers no doubt came out some twenty years before, just as their grandmothers did. There were some lovely ballgowns and many must have cost a small fortune. Of course they could be worn on more than one occasion, but those with a full season of balls to go to would have had many gowns …

But to be fair, for many of the young ladies this was a year of thrills and excitement, romance and fun, for they met their prince and married, to live happily ever after – while the fashion industry benefitted greatly as every garment worn, and their millinery, handbags, gloves and shoes, all will have been photographed for the newspapers and glossy magazines and studied avidly. The season meant high fashion; one came out in style.

In the fullness of time, after the ball, the finishing school term ended and there was a gathering of all the ladies for the Head to address before sending them, now finished, out into the world. Her eye alighted on a small parcel wrapped in tissue paper – clearly a gift for her; excellent! So she told them how they had come as unfashioned clay, but were now moulded; poised and polished; all her ladies could speak intelligently on any subject, and brilliantly on at least one. They had been fashioned and fired, wrapped in tissue paper and labelled secret – for some young man to come and undo! (I kid you not)

Well! You can imagine the peals of laughter from Lydia; she was helpless with mirth and found it impossible to keep a straight face. She was asked to leave the proceedings. The Head was not amused; in fact she was furious. But it was not ladylike to show excessive emotion and certainly not to show any loss of self-control. She remained dignified, a little remote, but charming while she accepted her leaving present. Having given this last little lesson on good manners, she smiled a small smile of condescension, looked down her nose at her transformed ladies, and left. Although only just over

5ft, she was always very good at looking down her nose at others – even a 6ft man! That is a very useful accomplishment to acquire.

One term was certainly enough to finish you off!

Rural Church Choir

Choir   We are the girls who sweetly sing in choir.
We regularly meet in church and come
from near and far.
We lift up our voices in notes of liquid gold
And some of us are young and lovely –
some of us are old.

Old lady   Thursday again and I must go to choir.
I'd much prefer to stay at home and
sit beside the fire;
I'll miss my favourite programme,
I know it's on the box –
I'd stretch out on the sofa and consume
a lot of chocs.

I have contemplated saying that I'm ill!
But you can bet your bottom dollar that
the vicar will
Call to see me later and tenderly enquire
If I'm now recovered? Oh! I'd better go to choir.

Choir Hark how we sing! Our voices fill the skies ...
We're all of us ambitious and we'd like
    to harmonise.
We want to sing at concerts – even broadcast
    on the air!
But no one ever asks us, don't know why;
    it isn't fair!

Vicar Thursday again and I must patient be
And grateful for the ladies who so kindly
    sing for me.
It's not King's College Cambridge whose music
    fills my ears ...
It's just my band of ladies as they do their best,
    poor dears.

TEENAGER IN THE 50s

"Are you smoking, Hannah?" Her voice was loud and accusatory.

"No, Ma'am," said Hannah, the smoke rising up behind her as she held the cigarette in cupped hands behind her back. "No, Ma'am." Looking at her straight in the eye. Soon, I reckoned, she'd burn her fingers, or set fire to her nylon apron. Nylon is highly flammable, I believe.

Ma'am was my mother; she did a 'huh!' with a stern look, then turned and left the room. We were in the servants' quarters, Hannah and I. Hannah was a cook, who could turn her hand to just about everything, cleaning or cooking. She was almost 5ft tall, with fiercely permed dark hair; a fierce face, along with some random moles that each sprouted a single hair. She had what looked like the beginnings, or remnants, of a moustache. But I don't mention them as I have one and had been mortified when it was suggested I had mine removed 'permanently by a professional'. What does one say? I died a thousand deaths. Conversations were always kept 'safe' as far as I was concerned since I made sure nothing personal was ever discussed … be it about one's body or one's thoughts.

Hannah was German and, although diminutive, a whirlwind of activity where work was concerned (she'd sweep and wash the kitchen floor each day, and wash the walls once a week).

It was a Friday evening and the parents were playing bridge with friends. As I had just arrived from London, I was directed to Hannah's quarters. At weekends bridge was often on the go, so it was normal to make oneself scarce. Hannah was always welcoming. She was also always smoking – though never in the kitchen, pantry etc.

She had a telly in her sitting room and greatly enjoyed wrestling, getting very involved in the holds and throws and clutchings and bitings … she'd shout encouragement and call on the combatants to kill each other if possible; and if not, at least to render them unconscious. I happily joined her as an almost-contestant and lent my loud yells and screams to hers: enjoyable joint audience participation. The parents disapproved of watching anything other than the BBC; they felt ITV was definitely lower class. Remember, this is in the early 50s; I think there were only two programmes then, in black and white.

Many people bought their first ever TV in order to watch The Queen's Coronation. If I recall correctly, that was in colour … but I only saw it as a film in a cinema. *God Save the Queen* was played at the end, so we all stood up. Then played again, so we all stood up again. At the third playing we gave up. But our first TV sets were untrustworthy and the picture would roll from top to bottom – endlessly rotating; and if we got the picture to stay steady, we lost the sound. So the choice was ours; sometimes one of us would sit by the set and twiddle knobs to catch a bit of both – picture and sound. The presenters wore black tie or evening dress – though, apparently that was only for their top half which was seen on screen. Legs could be in trousers and boots or skirts for the ladies.

There used to be potters with a wheel making pots for us all to watch during the gaps or intervals between programmes; or goldfish swimming about in a fishtank, which was pleasant. That reminds me of a dentist who had them in the waiting room; they were meant to calm us down as they swam around with their mouths open ... though it did look as if they couldn't remember what they were supposed to be doing. One day a fish had died, the dentist was upset and his hand shook. Then it didn't seem such a good idea.

There was a family dog; always a Labrador. One didn't take dogs for walks – or we didn't. There was plenty of space for it to run around in, or just follow us if we were going to the kitchen garden, or the maze (what was left of it; lot of work) or along the drive etc. The dog seemed perfectly fit, wasn't fat; appeared to be happy. Of course it wasn't fed on dog food, tins etc. It had lights occasionally and scraps. What are lights? Lungs. One black Lab liked to bury her bones, usually in the garden; however, on this occasion Hannah found the bone under her pillow – a nasty messy find. Perhaps the dog hadn't been able to get outside to do her burying. Or perhaps Hannah was dearly loved, or her pillow smelled as being of the right bone-burying material.

Hannah felt that if a dog or a child bit you, then you should bite them back and in theory they would never bite again. I think she did it with a dog ... but am not sure what a mother or father would say if they saw someone biting their child.

We went to London once a week by train. Father had his hair cut – he had very little; silver and shiny clean. Surely it can't have needed weekly attention? Perhaps he missed London, liked to be in the City, get back to his old, male dominated world ... have a break from us. I mean, it must be a shock to be in an office in a provincial town, not the City – he was making and taking decisions, knowing that what he did could be the difference between a business thriving or going under – and everybody's jobs dependent on you. A huge responsibility.

Lunch for him was in the City. The City was serious. It was Man's Business. One time he was looking so grave that someone on the next table said, "Cheer up, it may never happen." Father replied, "It already has." When he described what was troubling him (insurance wouldn't be paid on theft of lead guttering; it wasn't breaking in and entering), the colleague said it so happened he was a lawyer and the very fact that the thieves had put their fingers under the eaves to steal the lead meant they had broken in and entered. That was a very useful business lunch and encounter.

Mother would take me shopping and then to Harvey Nichols for lunch, where Jessie would serve us. Then we'd go to join Aunt Doris; she and Mother were at a convent school together. We'd meet at Harrods in the bank there ... lower ground floor. It was all tiles and great big green leather chairs and sofas. I loved it. And I loved Aunt Doris. She would like things Mother didn't like; and buy me things that Mother didn't think I needed ... notebooks, pens and pencils and so on. Dresses that Mother had decided didn't really suit me, Aunt Doris would pronounce perfect. She used to annoy Mother and I think she rather enjoyed doing so!

She was a little pouter pigeon of a lady; grey hair gathered on the nape of her neck, beautifully dressed and with very good posture. Upright with head held high. Her husband, not often seen as he stayed away from women shopping, always called her *Wife,* which greatly amused me.

London visits were often for me to go to the dentist; Father paid thousands on my teeth. Apparently they were very white and very weak. But every tooth had at least two or three stoppings; or was crowned. The dentist made a very nice living out of my teeth ... so much so that I was not surprised when I saw him in The Tatler having a posh society wedding. One had no way of knowing if the work was all necessary; but I suspect not. My parents felt that if we could afford any treatment ourselves, then we should pay for it; free health care etc. was for those less fortunate. Ditto scholarships.

Mother was tall and imposing and somewhat overweight in the tummy area; she'd say it was due to her operation(s). But she did like cream and chocolates etc. so would take slimming pills to counter any unwanted weight gain. She clearly felt it was her duty to give me a talk on sex when I was sixteen ... Father had gone for a walk and I'd said I'll come too; but he said, "No, stay with your mother, it will be nice for you to be together." So I'd smelled a rat and sat by the fire with my back to her. She referred to bees and butterflies going from one flower to another – and it is the same with people; thus she finished in a rush.

So, prepared for any bees and butterflies coming my way, I continued my life in happy ignorance. To be honest, in those days the greatest protection of all was fear, the fear of getting pregnant unwed. That kept one a virgin. The pill hadn't arrived then and when it was available, along came freedom and the possibility of sex for pleasure, not just for the production of children. I was astounded when a man, who'd been asked to make up a four with me at dinner by a couple, expected me to bed down after the meal – he was American and looked surprised when I'd said no thanks. But it's no different from eating and drinking and defecating, he said; just another thing we all do. Do we? No thanks.

Friends told me it was the fashion then to see how much you could have and enjoy without giving too much in return. Also that sometimes the man would say, "I won't take you out for a meal unless you agree to come to bed with me." As I didn't have a boyfriend till some years later, I was at no risk. Where was true love? Where was the prince who would conquer your heart and for whom you were saving yourself? One grew up on romance and one true love and waiting all one's life for that special person. Which reminds me of a young man who declared his love for me … I was pining after another young man I'd seen and hoped would ring and ask me out. He didn't. All weekend I would stay in, hoping he would ring. He didn't. Another wasted weekend, playing gramophone records (romantic Rachmaninov) and waiting. Having declined my swain's declaration and explained I thought I loved another, he left after saying he would always love me, never marry anyone else; would wait till I was eighty if need be ... how romantic was that!

Some months later he wrote to say he had meant every word, but he had now met somebody else and they were getting married shortly. He thought I'd like to know. I was still playing gramophone records, now moving on to Schumann – he could write some heart-rending music. Anyway, back to Mother ...

There was an occasion when she urged me to keep my virginity until I was married, this was very important. Also that my brother could not, or should not get married until I was wed. My brother was present at this conversation and was appalled; as I never got asked out to anything by anybody and looked like remaining a spinster for ever, his own prospects of a happy marriage had suddenly vanished.

It must have been about the same time that she took me to Harvey Nichols to get my first corsets. It was all hugely embarrassing, though the departmental floor lady, dressed in a little black dress, as they all were in those days, was tact personified. The corset was elastic and rayon? All in one like a swimming costume. I had to step into it, there were poppers in the bit between your legs. Very uncomfortable, there is no doubt a proper word for that part of the garment. You had to undo the poppers to spend a penny. At that first try-on session in the lingerie department I was asked to step in, bend forward and then lower myself into the thing. The little black dress lady kindly told me, "If I may say so, mademoiselle has a very lovely figure."

Oh! the embarrassment, the horror of it all. Given that I always had a capital H by my name at school to indicate

Heavy + (I was 9 stone at twelve and petite height-wise … it was only ever my height that was petite). But the lingerie lady had clearly been well trained in tactfulness.

Mother being about 5ft 10 seemed very tall to short folk. And, as she wore very high heels, she was of formidable stature. She always wore a hat when outside (everyone did) and Father was more than a little embarrassed by some of them. "Why did you let her buy that?" he would say. My only reply: "You should have seen the others!" He was a bundle of nerves and used to take Sanatogen. In the First World War he was a lancer in the cavalry. They rode horses in those days; now they ride in tanks. They were required to sniff gas so as to familiarise themselves with it should the Germans decide to deploy some. Unfortunately he took too big a sniff; as a result he was hospitalised, prostrate for a year. This was never referred to and I suspect his life was probably saved as a result. He was too old in the Second World War, although he may also have been unfit.

He joined the ARP (Air Raid Protection). I can remember the smell of burning and smoke when he came home one day holding a wooden drawer; which was burnt and had three singed ledgers in it; all that was left of his business. He would go on duty at various times during the day or night, holding his helmet and torch. A tall figure clad in navy off to do his bit for the nation.

During the war we learned useful patriotic songs such as:

> *Under the spreading chestnut tree Mr Churchill said to me*
> *If you want an air raid shelter free, join the*
> *bloomin' ARP.*

The ARP badges were made of silver.

> *Whistle while you work; Hitler made a shirt.*
> *Mussolini wore it, Churchill tore it,*
> *Whistle while you work.*

> *When the little pigs begin to fly, which is sure to*
> *happen by and by;*
> *Won't the country people stare at the bacon in the air –*
> *When the little pigs begin to fly.*

> *When the little pigs begin to fly, which is sure to*
> *happen by and by;*
> *We shall see the Duke of York in the season shooting pork –*
> *When the little pigs begin to fly.*

> *When the little pigs begin to fly, which is sure to*
> *happen by and by,*
> *We Britons will give in and ask Hitler to be King –*
> *WHEN the little pigs begin to fly!*

With apologies to whoever wrote the above; but we all sang them – very loudly.

Let it Rain

Let it rain. Let the water fall from heaven; let it rain.
Let the lightning flash and thunder crash,
> let the winds blow and water flow over me.

Let storms torment my body, let them lacerate my soul.
Let them batter, bruise and beat me until I feel my whole
Being rejoice in the glory of the elements' savage power.
Let the heavens open; unleash their might this hour.

Pour down, oh! ye waters! Batter the drowning trees;
Flatten the trembling earth; force it to its knees.
Blow ye mighty winds, blow! … hard and long and strong!
Carry all before you; howl your winter song.
Beat and bend and twist us – your destructive path must go
Across the world and ravage it.
> Blow ye mighty winds, blow!

Dark the night, the clouds. Starless, moonless the sky.
The world is desolation; alone on earth am I.

There, standing on the empty plain or on the lonely hill,
I breathe and live the power that is wind and rain until
I cry unheard above the storm to God to make it cease;
To help us in our helplessness: Oh! wind Oh! rain –
    be at peace.

Milking a Cow

Someone asked me if I knew how to milk a cow.
No problem, for of course I know and I shall
      teach you how.
So here's a helpful hint or two on what you need to do,
Lesson One is always fun: it's how to catch your moo.

Advance upon the beast holding sugar on the hand.
Say 'Down' or 'Heel' or 'Come here dear!' – be firm with
      your command.
Don't shout or move about in a way that gives alarm;
Milk goes sour within the hour if chased around the farm.

Take the ring that's in her nose and make the painter fast.
A sheepshank or a clove hitch – tie a knot designed to last.
Then take your stool – be calm and cool – drop anchor
      in the stall.
Hang her tail upon a nail or somewhere on the wall.

We don't want tails to swish in pails or get you in the eye.
Avoid cold hands – a cow demands warm fingers. So do I!
Then pat her flank and gently say some words
      of tender care.
Take your seat and squeeze a teat or two now, if you dare.

Remember cows are sensitive and some may be afeared
Of milkmaids with bright coloured hair or men who
        have a beard.
But milking's always easier – at least so I have found –
If the cow's asleep and you can keep her lying
        on the ground.

Now, all you milking men and maids,
        remember what you're told:
Take care it is the proper thing of which you're taking hold.
The cow's the one with bag astern. You know
        just what to do.
So try your best, you'll pass the test –
        but heaven help the moo!

Great Aunt's Recollections

He had run away to sea aged fourteen, sailing before the mast, changing his name and returning several years later as a man to join up and serve his country in the First World War Flying Corps. Having had 'a good war' (such an unpleasant phrase – not heard nowadays) he became much in demand as a single man to invite to the various house parties in large houses and stately homes. This was where they met, she being of the aristocracy. He not. These things mattered greatly then.

He was a handsome man who enjoyed the company of pretty girls; but she was the one he loved, wanted to be the mother of his children, and with whom he wished to be. Her mother-in-law was clearly less keen on the marriage. Once, when the last train had been missed to go back to London to her mother, the simplest thing to do was to stay the night and pop into her husband's bed. But her mother-in-law tried to get her to leave and go away. It was quite clear she was not wanted there. Then another female had arrived and was being made very welcome, very welcome indeed.

So alarm bells were ringing. She spotted an advert for a short cruise, the trip starting at Victoria Station. She arranged for her son to stay with her mother. Then she wrote to her husband giving him details of the cruise, saying she had two tickets – and she expected him to join her at Victoria Station at a certain time on a certain day. She heard nothing. On the day of departure, she went to the station and found her carriage. Sitting in it were her husband, hiding behind – I mean reading – a newspaper. Opposite him sat that other woman. No one said anything. Whistles blew, guards shouted, doors were slammed shut. Finally the woman stood up and said, "Are you going with her or coming with me?" No sound came from behind the newspaper. The other woman only just managed to get off the train as it started moving. I don't believe mention was ever made of the matter again.

The Second World War came and he was called back into service. The Royal Air Force. I don't imagine there was much money in those early married days, but as a young wife with a small boy she went with him and sought accommodation for them in the city, settling on a large house which had been converted into flats. She thought she could smell burning somewhere, though nobody else said they could. So one day, having sent her child out for a walk with the nanny, she rang the Fire Brigade. She enquired of the man who answered; "How much does it cost to hire a fire engine?"

He must have been somewhat surprised but asked why she wanted to know. So she said she could smell burning, though nobody agreed with her. A fireman on a motorbike came out, checked on the building and agreed – he could smell burning. There was a fire somewhere in the chimney which ran from top to bottom of the building. Fire engines, ambulances and police were all called to the scene. Apparently when the gas fires were added to the fireplaces on each floor, the builders had skimped on the concrete needed to protect the beams from any heat. A beam was smouldering, probably had been for days. When they broke into the chimney and the air got to it, the flames roared up; but being prepared, they quickly controlled the fire.

When the Battle of Britain began, she was organising the air force wives and got them digging up new potatoes in the fields while their husbands were engaged in dogfights high in the sky above.

Then he was needed in Canada and posted there. So she applied for and got the position of nanny to the two children of a Bank Manager who was sailing to Canada. She was determined to join her husband and keep the family together.

Alas, I do not know when she got the news – while on the ship, or on arrival? But her husband had been recalled to the UK and there was no way she could get back. So she spent the rest of the war in Canada. Those years were not wasted, however, as being a keen horse rider, astride or side-saddle, she instructed the Governor General's wife in the skills needed to ride side-saddle.

When the war ended, and they had been repatriated, they took up family life again. They both loved playing bridge, horse racing and going to the casino in Cannes. Bridge had been started at an early age; before she was seven … She was a good player and often very unconventional. That wasn't always easy for her partners, though they did say that bridge was exciting when played with her!

At one point, someone she had befriended at the bridge club called to see her as she was leaving the area. This good lady wanted to say goodbye and give her a thank you present. The gift was a pair of little ribbons with poppers attached to a small gold safety pin. These existed to help ladies keep their shoulder straps out of sight! Lots of straps, as petticoats were worn in those days ... and vests too! "Your straps are always showing," this lady said, "so I wanted to give you these and I hope they are a help!" Needless to say, they were never worn.

Great Aunt had ridden ever since she was a child, and she had her own horse when they lived in London – and her mother never knew about this. She was a good judge of horses, and racehorses in particular. As a couple, Great Aunt and her husband were always fun to be with; and at parties – if they weren't very enjoyable, the two of them would sit together and talk animatedly as if they had only just met. Parties were a burden to her young niece and she would join them to avoid having to make polite conversation – dressed in one of those (then) fashionable garments in brocade, with a huge black velvet bow at the rear and a skirt, full as a balloon, spread over a very scratchy net underskirt. Distinctly uncomfortable; particularly when sitting down. It had always seemed sensible, if you had to go to parties, to go in a horse box standing up so dresses weren't crushed.

Great Aunt had a cousin who dressed beautifully and would pass her frocks on. Having turned down an offer of a fur stole – mink? and not wishing to appear rude or ungrateful the niece felt she had to accept the offer of a second (no, that would be third) hand dress … although it was three or four sizes too big. Said Great Aunt, "Oh, just put a scarf in the neck and that will look fine."

"But what about all the cigarette burns on the bodice and halfway down the side of the skirt?"

"Oh, just cover what you can with your hand – and ignore the rest."

Right!

One Sunday when giving a lift to a friend after church she discovered she was being followed by some nasty looking men in a car. She couldn't shake them off and, on arriving home, she and her friend were too scared to leave the car. To their fright the men got out and came over – they then said they were police officers and her brake lights weren't working. Just to let her know! Great Aunt was furious, said they'd terrified her and they weren't dressed like police, but looked like thoroughly disreputable reprobates and should be ashamed of themselves.

When in their late sixties, her husband had a bad car crash. So for a rest and recuperation, they joined a cruise ship sailing out of Genova and on down to Naples. Amongst the passengers was an Italian family with children and a nanny, the father was English. One day Great Aunt saw the mother come in and look round anxiously as there was no sign of the nanny and children. So she told her husband to go and tell the mother that the children had gone to the swimming pool, no need for concern. Later, there was an invitation to join the family for drinks in their cabin.

The cruise ended and they were invited to come and visit the family in their palazzo in Rome. The taxi driver seemed reluctant to take them to the private entrance, but did so. Great Aunt couldn't help smiling as she put her white nylon M & S gloves on the butler's silver salver.

Great Aunt was a Character and her stories were fascinating, not least the tales about her own mother's early life and love. Her mother's uncle knew there was a suitor, and that his niece reciprocated. But they were on different echelons of the social scale. (Oh dear!) So our young man admired and yearned from a distance. The uncle, therefore, arranged a sailing trip for several family members and friends, so the two young people could see more of each other. But after a few days, our young man received a telegram saying he was needed back home. And he departed.

Sometime later the uncle met said suitor and exclaimed what a shame it was that he'd had to leave. The suitor then confessed that he couldn't bear to be near his love since he could never wed her, not being of good enough birth. So he had sent himself the telegram. At this the uncle said that his family all hoped the two of them would marry and that was precisely why they had both been invited to join the yacht! The young man was considered to be perfectly acceptable.

And so they did marry. But she was widowed early – another war – and remained a widow for 60 years. And Great Aunt grew up never really knowing her father.

Among Great Aunt's stories was one where she was staying with an aunt, Lady Tiddlypush, together with her young cousin from America. After an outburst about how unfair it was that her cousin couldn't have much fun, really enjoy herself, Lady T quietly asked her to ring for the butler. This she duly did, tugging the tapestried pull that hung to one side of the marble fireplace. The butler appeared, and Lady T told him to pack her American niece's belongings as she would be leaving that day and going to stay with Great Aunt (then aged fifteen!).

She, of course, had fifty fits … *What? I can't take her home with me?!!* etc. etc. Total panic! Said Lady T, "As you have had the temerity to question my actions regarding your cousin, you shall be in charge and she will be your responsibility. So she will leave now with you and be in your care."

Well, I suspect a lot of humble pie was eaten and many abject apologies made; and a lesson learned. Great Aunt's stories certainly brought alive another age – and how much things have changed. She was a one-off!

Snails ...

It may sound strange but I've grown to love the snail;
Such incredible creatures. I find they never fail
To enchant and amaze – for when I study one
Carefully, no matter what it's eaten or the damage done,
I find its striped shell beautiful – something to admire.

The yellows, the shiny conker-browns, the small ones
          red as fire ...
Along with big ones, mottled brown – which some folk
          like to eat.
All of them are stunning, and the tiny snails so neat
When newly hatched from eggs ... just perfect in every way
With little eyes on tentacles, that slowly move and sway
About – retracting swiftly when alarmed.
No; I would not wish to see them harmed.

We try to get rid of them most of the time –
They're eating our plants and veg, leaving slime
Everywhere ... horrid silver trails, unpleasant to see.

But thrushes enjoy snails and there, perhaps, we
Could help by letting them live, not be killed –
Certainly not by poisoning. Snails are filled,
With goodness, I'm told; we should preserve
Them for the thrushes and other birds which deserve
Consideration.

In truth, we should care for the many creatures with whom
> we share this world.

My Crime

Yes, I am a murderer – but no one knows my crime.
I did it – because I wanted to. And now I feel it's time
To tell the world of my success. It wouldn't be appreciated
Unless I told how I removed the person whom I hated.

He was an ordinary sort of chap, didn't often speak.
Used to ring one of the bells, went to church each week.
I hated him and his holy ways, I wished him into hell –
For every Sunday he was there, tugging at his bell,
His thin face eager, animated, joy lighting up his eyes
As if he saw Salvation? or found hope? up in the skies …

I decided I would kill him – quite why I do not know;
I only knew I hated him. The man had got to go.
I thought it all out carefully, no killings or of that sort.
Death must look accidental so the coroner's report
Would be Death by Misadventure. I knew what I would do.

I climbed to the top of the tower – and he kindly
        came up too.
Then I hit him hard till unconscious and shut him
        in the room
With all his blasted bells! They made a fitting tomb!

Soon after that, the bells were rung – and I listened below
    with glee.
Those bells were oh! so very loud, they almost deafened me!
And he was up there with the bells …too dazed to shout
    or cry:
Oh! how I laughed as they drove him mad and slowly
    made him die!

THE NANNY

She was there when they collected the child – a sister for the little girl who had already joined the family. For the parents, after several years of marriage but no babies, took the kind and courageous decision to adopt. This took some months – nowadays years – to arrange.

The couple evidently felt it was a reflection on them in some way not to have had children of their own. So the adoption was kept secret; they moving house and starting a new life as a family of four. However, as they continued to play golf at the same Club, it was obvious that the previously childless couple suddenly had two – and a nanny.

Years passed and the parents eventually employed several domestics in the shape of a cook and a maid. Also a gardener and a chauffeur. However, the maid fell pregnant; apparently the same man got several local lasses pregnant. It was after the war and there were suddenly many (handsome) young men living in the area. Not realising the situation, the daughter of the house – now sixteen – asked the poor pregnant maid why she was thin really, but her tummy so large? Not very helpful.

Now the cook, who was foreign, had had a child. But being unmarried, the boy was brought up by a married sister. So the aunt was his mother and his mother became his aunt. The real situation remained a secret. When the lady of the house found the maid was pregnant she had to pretend she'd had children and knew all about pregnancies. Whereas the cook, who had had a child, was pretending she hadn't, and that she knew nothing about such things. It all became a rather complicated situation. But the various pretences remained in place and local health organisations and charities eventually took charge of both the maid and the babe.

A sad little footnote; the cook's son came to see her when he learned the facts of his birth. He arrived to say that unless she gave him money he would tell everyone the truth.

The nanny eventually moved on to care for other babies. She had been courting and walking out with her young man for several years, but the First World War came along and she lost her fiancé. She always said she could never, ever consider courting anyone else. Throughout her life she looked after many babies. Years later, the now middle-aged girl met up with her old nanny and they would have lunch together in London. Lyons Corner House, 14s and 6d for a three course meal. Prawn cocktail, joint of beef or lamb or pork with peas, carrots and potatoes etc. Followed by ice cream/trifle! Delicious! The nanny always bought the girl a treat – a cherry liqueur chocolate.

Eventually the nanny went to live in a retirement bungalow. And, having been abroad some years, the girl went to visit her, staying overnight occasionally. Although the nanny had been given a good pension by more than one employer, she never spent the money, but kept it under the bed in a tin box. She saved electricity by not using the bathroom light – there was a streetlamp outside the window which she thought quite sufficient.

She told the girl that she was her favourite baby, the one she had always loved the most. The nanny had always given her total, unquestioning love. She'd creep upstairs with cups of sweet milky tea when the girl was 'naughty' and had been sent to bed in disgrace. "Why were you so naughty, dear?" Once, when the girl was staying with her she heard the nanny getting down on her knees, slowly and painfully, to say her nightly prayers. She thanked the Lord for bringing the girl back into her life, "I always knew she'd grow up lovely."

I Don't Get Many Letters

I don't get many letters now … people don't seem
>to write somehow.

They use those emails, on the internet. But I, for one, just
>cannot get

On with computers. When I try to write I suddenly find it's
>vanished from sight.

Daily doses of so called 'junk mail',
>all unsolicited noisily sail

Through the letterbox in the kitchen door,
>scattering themselves over the floor.

Leaflets in various shapes and sizes promise me
>wins with super prizes.

And then I'm warned of possible harm …
>surely I need a personal alarm?

And why not pay for my funeral to come …
>leaving till later could increase the sum.

Perhaps I need carers, with kind friendly faces,
        who'll cook (and wash those difficult places
I can't seem to reach)? They'd dust and should be a
        wonderful help to an old lady – me.
Then there are care homes, which look very nice,
        but if I delay or say I'll think twice
I may be too late … till another soul dies.

Oh! It's all such a worry and I now realise
I cannot decide, I haven't a clue – so it's best to do nothing!
        Yes, that's what I'll do!

Our Church – all churches closed in the Lockdown

I wonder if she's lonely, our little church … she's only
Open once a week for those who seek her quiet peace.
But loyal ladies never cease to dust, polish and clean.
       Our church is seen
As loved and cared for still.

For centuries, through good and ill,
Whether happy or sad, many or few, people have prayed,
       sung, knelt in pew;
Sought comfort and help amidst their tears …
       asked for courage to conquer fears
Of flood or drought, of death or disease.

Man thinks he controls all he sees …
He doesn't; so he comes to pray for help and guidance,
       to find a way
Of coping when distressed or pained. Throughout the ages
       the church remained
A sanctuary for those in need.

One day, when present ills recede,
People will gather here to sing, and church bells
            everywhere will ring.
While organ music again will sound as Christmas carols
            are sung around
The tree. For now, these days, our church has ceased her
            hymns of praise.

No breezes stir the cloistered air… no footsteps sound
            on belfry stair,
No organ player, nor bell ringer brings life to the bells;
            no voice sings.
The nave is empty, like chancel and pew; the pulpit
            unpeopled, the altar too …

But here, for centuries, the faithful prayed;
            the place with prayer is overlaid.
You enter to find an old church where it is not empty,
            but filled with prayer.

School Days
1943—1949

The happiest days of your life, they say; and one can see why. Even if you hated those days, they were still special because you were still young. Though there was nothing to hate really. Having been fortunate to be evacuated to beautiful countryside during the worst of the bombing, going to a prep school in the country meant a wonderful start to life.

The actual building must have been a pleasant Georgian house standing in its own grounds near Virginia Water. To our young eyes it seemed very large. There were many well established trees and they were all named, so that as you walked past them a small label on the ground gave you their English and Latin titles. A brilliant way of learning. There was a fire escape on the front of the house; apparently one potential mother who'd visited to inspect the school saw it and asked what it was. On being told, she said, "Oh, if you're expecting to have fires, then I shan't send my daughter here."

At the beginning of term everyone went to Matron to

have their hair inspected for lice. I was never aware of anyone having them, though I'm told they were – are – rife; they like clean hair.

The very little girls were woken up at about 10 pm and 'potted' before being put back to bed; one was almost asleep throughout, not really waking up. The floors were all either dark green lino or wooden floorboards; there were no carpets, except in the Head's sitting room which one visited on a Sunday evening – to sew and behave nicely – and the odd small rug by each bed in the dorms.

The girls took it in turns to fill metal jugs with hot water from the bathroom and put one outside each bedroom door at seven in the morning. Those jugs nowadays would appear to be antiques and of some value; rarely seen. Then everyone went for a run before breakfast which was at eight. One time it was foggy so they chatted for a while and then cut across the grounds to arrive panting at the finish. They hadn't realised that a member of staff was with them in the fog; they were all told to do it properly. After everyone had made their bed, school started at nine; assembly with prayers first.

Prayers daily in the morning, and again in the evening with a hymn sung and then quiet reading until it was your turn to leave the room and go upstairs to bed. On Sundays it could be three lots of praying in a day; but if there was singing, she enjoyed it. At school they were allowed two photos on the bedside table and she had a black and white photo of the daughter of her parents' friends. On arrival, the head of the dorm saw it and said, "Is that your bosom friend? Oh, but you haven't got one to have one, have you." What a way to start one's first day at school; difficult anyway as, not having a tie, her mother had sent her in wearing a woollen jumper instead of a shirt. To make matters even worse, her dead straight hair was always parted on one side and there was a big silk bow on the other. Matron was now called upon to inspect said bow, watch it being tied by her mother and then practice doing it. Totally mortifying … Needless to say, ribbons and bows were soon ditched for elastic bands.

Everyone wore them as your hair must not reach as far as your shoulders; then bunches were the order of the day. Plaited wonderful braids for those who had long and lovely hair.

Skirts of daily uniform must just touch your legs when you knelt; Sunday skirts were longer. White socks when young; then long grey socks. And finally Lisle stockings (known as concretes) when you were grown up. Suspenders needed for them! Awful!

There were games in the afternoon, and/or walks in Windsor Great Park. Once a week there was an hour of singing and also an hour of musical appreciation when the teacher played gramophone records of classical music. Gym weekly with really good equipment; a bar for walking/balancing along, a big leather horse for vaulting, a rope for climbing up, wall bars for other challenges. The chance to get and keep fit; exercises we all had to do. It was good. You had to play games each afternoon, except Sundays; if you didn't play, you had to be outdoors and watch and/or walk. Special treats were walking to watch The Royals change from a motor car to the open carriage pulled by the Windsor Greys when they went to Ascot; also a visit to St George's Chapel – this left the writer with a passion for music and architecture.

Walks with a picnic by the Copper Horse and the Long Mile; preferably with hard boiled eggs! Once, they found the eggs were raw; so spread the word rapidly – Don't eat egg!

Before breakfast, everyone lined up to show their hands for inspection by a teacher; nails clean and then turned over to show the palms. Not sure they didn't look at their necks too.

In the dining room sliced bread was put out the night before on a metal tray, and covered with a damp teacloth. There was reconstituted egg, which was watery and unappetising. A single boiled sweet – one each – was passed round after Sunday lunch. When one course was finished you showed your empty plate to the teacher at the head of the table. Particularly noisome things like greens and tapioca were often not consumed – so someone with a clean plate would lend it to others to put over their uneaten food for the teacher to inspect. Piles of uneaten food would sometimes appear on the side table (or under our table on the floor). On more than one occasion, a teacher spotted this when everyone rose for grace prior to leaving the dining room; they were then made to get the food, return to table and eat it. They had to stay there until it had all been consumed, no matter how long it took. Food was special; not to be toyed with nor treated lightly; we were very lucky to have it. Many in the world were starving, we would be reminded.

Once, having obviously upset her seniors, she was hung on the clothes hooks by the lockers with a bar of soap in her mouth. Everyone wore overalls for meals and it was this garment she was wearing when this assault on her liberty took place. It took a while for some stitching to give way and for her to fall to the ground. She was late for the meal – but, when asked why, did not say. It would probably have brought another punishment. At age seven the ten year olds seemed very big and the twelve year olds really old, almost like grown-ups.

Netball and rounders and tennis were all played, when the weather allowed. If rain or snow prevented this the girls danced with each other learning Scottish reels and also how to do the foxtrot, waltz and polka; this equipped them if called upon to dance later on in life.

There was also a large covered area, sides open to the air, where jacks were played, skipping, hopscotch, all manner of activity could take place if wet or snowy. Swimming in summer was a visit by coach to the public baths in Richmond. The two hours were reserved for them and some members of staff. And a boiled sweet each was dished out at the halfway point on our return journey.

Church on Sunday was a forty-five minute walk through the countryside for an hour's service, then back. They each had a penny to put in the collection. This came from a sum they started the term with – supplied by parents – and a small account book was kept with the cash box. This was filled in meticulously and served to start them on careful spending, and the recording of credit and debit. Sometimes the Head would say 32d and five buttons had been put in the collection; this was when some naughty older girls tried to keep a few pennies in order to buy sherbet powder. There was a little shop over the fence where the walks started; it was very daring to climb over it, make a purchase and get back.

She didn't dare.

There were good causes to support and sometimes the house mistress would say they had not made a very generous donation – and required them to increase it. Weekdays they rested on their beds for half an hour after lunch. On Sundays it was serious reading (Dickens and Goldsmith) for an hour after lunch, before going for a walk in a crocodile.

Everyone had a small square of garden, in which to grow veg and flowers. Excellent idea.

Two baths a week – Matron came in to scrub backs – three inches of water allowed. Hairdressers came once a fortnight to wash hair, leaning forward over a hand basin in a very uncomfortable position. Towel dried plus gas stove to kneel in front of … with an adult present in case of fire.

The teachers were all, save the science teacher, women. Misses Mudd, Root, Reed, Flint and Stone. You wouldn't believe it! There was an elderly couple, she was probably a housekeeper while he did maintenance and so on; and when there was a fancy dress competition they went as each other, wearing one another's clothes and, for her hair, he used that grey wire wool everyone scoured aluminium saucepans with. They won!

There were netball and tennis games and matches, which sporty girls enjoyed. They despised the academic girls, who no doubt despised them in turn. There were Brownies dancing round toadstools … learning knots, first aid and useful skills (*proficiencies:* they got badges and then sewed them on the arms of their uniform); *'We're the Brownies here's our aim; lend a hand and play the game'*. She did it whole heartedly and thought Brown Owl and Tawny Owl were wonderful.

Then she flew up to become a Girl Guide and was amazed to find they'd gone on strike; when Captain blew her whistle everyone vanished into the bushes surrounding the field, not reappearing until 'guides' was over. Why they did this she can't recall. But she was shocked. She was a prig. (Still?)

One girl told a smaller one that she was her sister who had been stolen by gypsies some years previously. This got back to the Head and then the parents concerned – there were ructions.

The same girl told her class she was going to commit suicide one sunny afternoon; so they all watched in wide eyed terror mixed with awe and some excitement. Don't tell a teacher until I am dead. No; they wouldn't. Evidently the girl had found some iodine, pretended to drink it, smeared it on her mouth ... then did some gradual shaking, and shivering and jerks and spasms, along with some moans and dramatic groans. She was obviously a very good actress – and with her vivid imagination, probably went on to write books. How the performance ended has been forgotten!

There was one occasion when two girls were practising some press ups together in the dorm and a teacher saw them, jumped to the wrong conclusion and told them to report to the Head at once; they could expect to be expelled immediately. Fortunately, the head girl was nearby and went to see the Head; the teacher was expelled. The girls knew they were being naughty by talking, which wasn't allowed in the dorms.

In scripture lessons when they read aloud from the bible words like womb, conceive and breast caused acute embarrassment. So much so that one after another the girls would say they had lost the place and were unable to read that verse; this would go on till the teacher realised there was a problem.

The Facts of Life were dealt with if you studied biology (bilge). If not, then there was a little talk with your House Mistress before leaving the school. She chose her words carefully and explained that when a man and woman married and wanted to have a baby, part of the man went into part of the woman. While saying this, she demonstrated by holding her right hand palm up – rather as if she was offering a lump of sugar to a pony. Then she lifted her hand and moved it up, over and down to fit snugly between the palm and thumb of her left hand. Kind of like shaking hands with herself.

So that was all quite clear then.

Twice a term their parents could take them out for lunch on Sunday. Girls were expected to wear their hat … all the time, I think; but that didn't happen. Having gone to a hotel for lunch one time she'd gone to the ladies room. There were those big brass doorknobs and a huge shiny rectangular thing with a slot for the one penny charge which would allow access. On closing the door it would change from vacant to occupied. A purse taken in one time, but forgotten when she left, meant climbing back over the top of the door; this took some doing – fortunately there was a gap between the top of the door and the ceiling. But then the door could not be opened from the inside as no penny had been put in, so she had to climb over again to get out. This also took some doing – and got her some very strange looks from the grown-ups powdering their noses.

They really did powder them in those days, looking into a little compact with the powder and a mirror. So if you wanted to spend a penny, you said you were going to powder your nose. At school you said you wanted to be excused.

This must all seem very dull and unexciting. But it was towards the end of the war; blackout blinds were still everywhere. There were no televisions or gramophones at school; they could read (a suitable book), knit and/or sew. You made your own entertainment. There would be few cars about. We didn't go to the shops – it wasn't allowed anyway, and we did not have money other than for church, good causes etc.; besides, we had everything we needed. If a parent sent some chocolates, they had to be handed over and were then issued to her one square a day – once a girl ate the entire bar in one go to stop Matron taking it.

We were so lucky with the beautiful grounds, where you walked, or played games or sat and read; Windsor Park, which was wonderful, where everyone walked – always accompanied by a teacher; hearing for the first time classical music played on gramophone records by the teacher; group singing and choir practice. 'Nymphs and Shepherds Come Away', which is now appreciated and still makes everyone roar with laughter. These were all quiet, safe and good days and ways to start learning; to start life. They were happy years.

Thames Tributary

We went for a walk by the river, my friends and I;
We wondered what fish, what birds we'd espy.
Who knows, there might be the kingfisher's gleam
Of turquoise as it flashed along the stream.
Or we might hear the moorhen's contented call …
We saw plastic aplenty; wildlife? None at all.

Seagulls and swans were there on the lake;
Lovely to see, but to lift the heart and make
Us glad would be to see the heron or coot,
Or water disturbed as ducklings shoot
Into the reeds to hide. So little to see
Or hear. Just discarded plastic everywhere. We
Should be ashamed.

The Estuary in Autumn

Where estuary meets the countryside gulls and ducks
    in small flocks ride
The waves – feathered flotillas. On the beach beyond
    the latest tidal reach
The strand is edged with, mainly man-made, litter;
    and there it has stayed
With washed-up wood, drying on stones, bleached like
    long-abandoned bones.

Small birds harvest the autumn hedge and from the
    reed-filled marsh the sedge
Warbler, with his scratchy song, tells us that it won't be long
Till autumn's season comes to an end. The curlews call,
    their haunting songs send
Sad memories over the water. With stately stride they now
    patrol the turning tide
While, in newly uncovered mud, they seek fresh food
    with down-curved, probing beak.

A heron, motionless, fixes his eye on fish or eel,
    while in trees nearby
The little egrets watch – looking like white hankies
    in the branches. By night
There are owls and foxes, badgers too. But all too rarely
    the nightingale, who
Sings his song to the star-filled sky. Occasionally otters
    will come by.

Along secluded creeks are stunted oaks, twisted and gnarled,
    where green moss soaks
Up moisture. In nearby meadows cattle graze,
    while flocks of sheep with lambs spend days
On short clifftop turf. The fields of grain, once golden
    in the sun, have again
Been harvested and red-brown soil is now in furrows as
    screaming gulls follow the plough.

Secretarial College 1950s

Going to live in London to learn shorthand and typing at a secretarial college was the first time I'd lived away from home in a bed and breakfast establishment. Three or four girls in a room. The floors were the usual dark green lino; this sweeps easily to keep clean. Breakfast supplied by a capable woman who kept an eye on us all. There was a handbasin in the bedroom; loos on the half landings, which were shared by all. Food was not allowed in the bedrooms. We were allowed our gramophones and records. I had ten.

South Kensington had one of the first Italian coffee bars; wonderful places with – was it Gaggia? – hissing noisily as it produced fresh coffee. Espresso. The bars in Soho were apparently the 'in' thing and crowded out. We knew nothing of Soho. Ours, thankfully, was quiet and safe and we girls would go there and spend an hour and a half over one coffee, smoking (we had learned to do this – cigarettes being cheap then) and discussing everything and nothing. Politics seems to have been far simpler in those days. There weren't so many of them for a start.

How we knew what was going on in our country, let alone the world, I don't know. Unless one bought a newspaper (one didn't), or went to the cinema (rarely) – that was a world of muscled men smiting a massive gong; there were cockerels crowing, lions roaring, Pathé news etc. Usherettes with torches showed you to your seat and there was a newsreel followed by a short film and then the main feature. This had an interval halfway through when the lights came up and the usherettes sold sweets and ice creams. At the end of the programme, everyone stood up for the national anthem. But over time, people began leaving before the end of the film in order to 'get away'. There were also news cinemas, half an hour or thereabouts of repeated news throughout the evening. So where did one get any news from? I expect we didn't bother. There'd be headlines writ large and displayed on the boards by the newspaper sellers on the streets; they'd shout the latest news and keep us informed, willy nilly. Maybe, because the war was over, we were all happy and enjoying every moment, despite rationing continuing. Life was good. Life was fun.

Anyway at the secretarial college there were about twenty girls, living in shared accommodation nearby, with bed and breakfast. Other meals you had to eat out – this meant cheap fry ups in cafes, Lyons? Then back to the bedsits – and listening to gramophone records. All classical, as far as I was concerned. Our evening entertainment was having friends in (girls) to listen to records.

The phone in the entrance hall of our digs was a public one, which devoured much money when used; those pennies, florins etc. being very large and heavy compared with coins today. Really, it was for emergencies only. Another money-eater was the gas fire; 1/- a time, the meter had to be fed all evening. We often wore our heavy outdoor woollen coats indoors.

It doesn't sound wildly exciting; but it was our first experience of 'being an adult' and in charge of our own lives. Pitman's shorthand was studied, learnt and practised till it became automatic, almost unthinking. We'd been told it was easier to learn if you weren't too clever and could just be a conduit of the heard word onto the page. Of course you needed to be able to read it back … and to type fast, non-stop, meant having earpieces and turning up the volume if you were typing recorded dictation so you could hear over the clatter of your typewriter, which probably contributed to later deafness. It was slower if you listened to a phrase, typed it, then listened to the next few words, and so on.

A lunch break of a sandwich nearby. Then back to the typing, on big upright Imperial or Royal machines, we all bashed away in time to Charlie Kunz who played the piano at a steady tempo … for hours, and days on end! The gramophone was electric so it wasn't having to be wound up by hand by the teacher; the records were the 10 inch and 12 inch 78 rpm heavy duty sort. Not LPs in those days. The aim was to touch type and get you going faster … no stopping to look for the letters and then back at the manuscript.

This was a year of study, prior to setting forth in the wide world to seek work. But somehow I'd met Miss Frith, also living in the boarding house, who had sung with Dame Clara Butt, who had sung in front of Their Majesties at Buckingham Palace. As music was my passion, we had shared records and listened to them together. She introduced me to the *Brandenberg Concertos*. Told me her life had been as part of a choir. They all had to practise and rehearse and keep to the regime required – but not Clara, who never practised but just stood up, opened her mouth and sang – fabulously. Very annoying. One of my first records was of her singing *Abide with Me*. Another precious record was of *Solemn Melody* – Walford Davies. This I'd played to my mother who said it made her feel suicidal and forbade me to play it again. I've still got those first 78 records, amongst which Kathleen Ferrier and Isobel Baillie singing two gorgeous duets …

So in quiet South Ken the year long secretarial course came to an end and I moved into a bedsit near Harrods while I took temporary work. Actually on the buying side of Harrods, where I managed to deliver lingerie in the shape of combinations to the department selling hairbrushes etc. The delivery note said 'Combs'. Which I thought meant combs … not combinations. There were two underground floors at Harrods; one was where all the refrigerated rooms were for storing ladies furs during the summer. And one was full of packing cases, big cardboard boxes where there were Jamaicans beating and playing the boxes like drums – and singing. It was such a lovely surprise.

The bedsit I had moved to had a hand basin, and one had the use of a lavatory, and the kitchen for breakfast only. This bedsit also had dark green lino flooring. The hand basin was boxed in, and when I explored it there was a handgun inside. A Luger. I put it back. The frying pan on the stove would have congealed fat in it from the previous night. Sometimes there were mice footprints in it. I didn't ever have a cooked breakfast.

On one occasion friends and I went to the Queensway skating rink near Bayswater. We had our own skates because every winter the family used to skate on the frozen pond at High Beeches ... which was great fun. I wonder if it still freezes there in winter as it did in the forties? But in London I wore trousers to go skating, the first pair I had ever owned. The parents were horrified; girls didn't wear trousers, let alone unaccompanied after dark. It was winter, male escorts should really be present. (I agree! It would be lovely but I didn't have any)

Certainly, there were times when my friends and I accompanied each other home ... then felt nervous of going back alone ... and in the end we'd dash onto different underground trains and go our separate ways. On one occasion we noticed two men following us; we hopped off the train, so did they; we hopped on again ... they did too ... eventually we managed to get on before they could.

One time, having arranged to meet at 6pm outside Swan and Edgar at Piccadilly Circus, I was on the street while my friend was at the entrance from the underground. We'd waited some time before deciding to check on the different levels and find each other. But I got told to move on; beginners wait the other side. What beginners? Eventually, I twigged on.

Dressing up always dismayed me as it was synonymous with being uncomfortable. High heels, perhaps low by many standards, but still high to me. Tried on for five minutes in a carpeted high class establishment was not the same as walking pavements all day, nor being at parties for hours.

As it was the fashion to wear big, full skirts and dresses – material now being available, I was dressed accordingly. Once I actually fell for, really coveted, a full circle skirt. It was super.

Red felt, with black flamingos all round the hem. I loved it – so much so that, to my shame, I spent my week's accommodation money and bought it. Then I hadn't got the flat rent money; out of desperation I contacted a friend of my brother and went to The City by tube to meet him and get the cash. This meant saving up to repay him, which I did by spending no more than 1/- a day on food for several weeks. Weeks were five days only, because I went home weekends. A return rail ticket to Reading was £9, which I had difficulty funding sometimes as I must have made some unnecessary or foolish purchases.

Looking back at our clothes then, you always wore stockings, or later, tights. High heels, gloves, hat, and a costume or suit. Watching Wimbledon in summer was a challenge; don't forget, we had petticoats on as well. When at home you got up in a skirt; changed into jodhs to go riding. Changed back to the skirt. And changed again for supper – or dinner, which on Saturday meant black tie.

A man's tweed suit, made to measure, cost 14 gns. A sheepskin coat £12 – handmade. You could choose the label you had sewn on; Fortnum and Mason, Harvey Nichols, etc.

It seems unbelievable that when I earned 8 guineas a week the head of the agency said it called for a drink as I was then the highest paid person she had on her books. Petrol was 4/6 a gallon; the forecourt attendant served you, cleaned the windscreen and then you tipped him. If you belonged to the AA the patrol man on his motorbike and sidecar would salute you on seeing your badge on the front of your car.

My brother would drive us back to London on a Sunday evening; there must have been a wireless as we would have Palm Court Hotel on and sing to all the songs. The journeys were alright then, so there must have been far fewer cars. Of course there were – streets in towns were two-way traffic, plus parking. Those now are one-way, with parking on one side. Look at the size of the Austin 7 or Morris Minor 1000 compared with some of the huge cars now. We had little orange arrows that flicked out as indicators; our headlights were not so bright and glaring – and many a car needed its starting handle to cope with cold winters. When the windscreen wipers stopped functioning, I tied string to them and in through the windows on both sides of the car; as the passenger it was my job to pull them from side to side to make them work. Hideous smogs rendered London impossible to navigate; the passenger leant out of the window to look at the pavement and direct the driver. Or had to get out and walk in front of the car. Terrifying; you literally could not recognise where you were. Our clothes were filthy; collars, cuffs and hems. Black.

Brother would lend me his car in the evenings if he didn't need it. It was a two-seater and I'd get a friend to join me and then, if it was a lovely night, we'd go for a two or three hour drive. Once we drove to Southend, and just as we arrived all the street lighting went out. So I parked, carefully as I thought. A policeman appeared and inspected us with a torch and said, "Hello Ladies." He then showed us that we had parked amongst some roses growing on the middle of a roundabout. We apologised and he helped us reverse off and back onto the road. He said he reckoned we were nurses who'd been on nights and needed a break.

Enough of reminiscences: we had fun, and life was really quite uncomplicated. We were fortunate. But then came the fear of nuclear war. That fear was very real.

Aftermath

The dying sun is sinking at the fading of the year.
There's a coldness to the twilight, a glimpse of pale grey fear.
The silver-plated sky, now dull, is glazed like blinded eyes;
While the air is silent, still, and dead; the world in ruin lies.

The dirty silver horizon where a fearful sun has fled,
Sinking, drowning, falling – and dying with the dead.
The houses are deep in shadow – their lights
        no longer gleam –
They huddle abandoned, wrecked – in a frozen
        silent scream.

The uneasy skyline's jabbed and stabbed where cruel
        church spires stand;
A terrible air of death and doom hangs over
        this blighted land.
A haunting, evil presence, an ominous 'something' felt
While the clammy fingers of fear write out the words
        that death has spelt.

No distant laughing voices now; no people, animals, sound.
No sign of life or movement; no waters seaward bound.
Just dark, dead, rotten grasses that are odorous and black
Beside the stagnant, stinking waters, rank and slimy, slack.

The trees are hideously twisted, so gnarled and deathly cold.
Their petrified branches bare and leafless,
> frightful to behold.
And overhead, threatening, cruel, above this blighted place
Are storm-charged, grey-black angry clouds writhing
> their way through space.

The land is changed and terrible – now blasted,
> bleak and sad.
Deaf and mute, crippled and blind; numbed and maimed
> and mad.
Without colour, without sound, without life,
> without breath;
Just silent, still and stopped: given over to death.

The Owl

Twilight is falling across the land
Spreading to where the old trees stand,
And shadows are thrown on the woods below –
The shining moon lets her silver flow.

Birds are now silent – a creature may howl;
But soft as ever is the owl,
Soundlessly winging her way through the night,
Brushing by with a touch so light
That one starts and hearts beat high
To see her, dreamlike, drifting by.

The watchful, motionless trees are still
While the hunter quarters the ground until
She finds her prey. With feathered ease
She flies; as soft and silent as the breeze.

TESSA OF ROME

It was a shock to me when I learned that Tessa was actually about fifty, when I was mid-twenties.

She apparently dyed her hair, which I hadn't realised, so she always looked about thirty – she was auburn and had a double barrel surname, belonging to an old Irish family. We met when she called on my boss as they were evidently old friends. So that was nice for him as he'd just arrived in Rome to take up a new post.

Unfortunately, she broke her leg and was confined to her flat, on the outskirts of Rome, and I was asked to rally round and look after her. So inevitably we got to know each other and became friends. Remarkable, given that my cooking was limited to fry ups and that is what I fed her on every day.

It transpired that Tessa broke her leg trying to stop a bottle of milk from falling over in the well of the passenger seat. She instinctively reached out with one hand while driving with the other – and hit the wall where she parked her car. Tessa was frail, which was why she drove everywhere as walking was an effort and made her breathless. She was minus a lung and a collarbone due to TB.

Her mother had left Tessa's father and taken her three daughters to northern Italy to live on the Ligurian Coast; apparently this was much cheaper than the UK and they could live there on £60 a year – and have a lovely climate too.

When the TB occurred, I'm not sure, but she was in hospital in Gstaad and patients were wheeled out in their beds to be on the balconies and breathe the (very cold) fresh air. Tessa's first visit back to the UK when she was well enough to travel was just before the Second World War broke out, so she was never able to return to Switzerland to complete her treatment. As I said, she was frail.

By coincidence, having broken my leg skiing I was in the same hospital in Gstaad some twenty plus years later. They had twelve legs a day coming in; I'd got stuck in some icy ruts and one ski point got caught and crack, my foot was facing backwards. A four hour wait on the mountainside and then the sledge (blood wagon) journey down to the hospital. The fittings didn't have safety release mechanisms then and they seem very old fashioned now, as do the ski boots. If anyone's interested, I skied happily for many years afterwards – with lovely modern boots.

But back to Tessa in Rome with her leg in plaster, and receiving daily fry ups from me. I'd drive over during the lunch hour (three plus hours actually) to find her poking a long knitting needle down the plaster to try and stop an itch. Or, on another occasion, struggling with a pair of scissors – kitchen scissors for cutting up poultry – and had started to cut through the plaster with the aim of removing it. Anyway, eventually she recovered and we took to going for drives in the country when I finished work at one o'clock on a Saturday. We'd take a picnic and go up into the hills – find a village with vineyards, park in a field gateway and enjoy the views and goats and so on. Not forgetting the snakes, to beware of. We'd look at the old palazzi and the churches; the narrow streets often winding uphill to a piazza in front of the church. Too narrow for cars, and walking was an effort for Tessa, so usually I'd do the visiting and then recount to her all I had seen.

We visited some stunning old churches and buildings and wonderful roofs in terracotta tiling, which are a delight to look down on from a height. We'd quench thirst from the fountains and spouts that were everywhere for everyone to help themselves to. The men sitting in the shade outside the local osteria, always playing cards. No women in sight, for they sat outside their houses sewing and lace making. Married women facing the street; the unmarried maidens facing the house, maintaining their modesty. They were all, always, dressed in black, with their heads covered. No woman ever wore trousers. That would be Westerners from the big cities, who also wore make up. Only with your brother could or would you be out after dark; foreigners did so, and were considered loose women.

A stout lady bearing some handfuls of long grass, with a stick in the other hand, slowly walked a large pig up the street, tapping and steering him/her onward till they reached the piazza. There the grass and pig were put in the shade of the church to spend the afternoon. The stout signora slowly returned home; far too hot to do anything in a hurry.

On one excursion the car misbehaved and it seemed a good idea to seek help in the village. Apparently there was a mechanic there and he showed us to his mother's house where we were given a bowl of warm water and soap, along with a towel, so we could clean up after our efforts under the car bonnet. Then we were given a glass of the local wine and chatted while the car was put right. Altogether a very pleasant experience, and later to our embarrassment they would take no payment as they said they had so enjoyed meeting us.

Similarly, at the cobbler's one day, he would take no payment but said it's nice to have something free occasionally and today there's no charge. So many good, kind people; I still think of them.

Once, up in the Abruzzi mountains, spending a weekend there, we were told in the village that Maria the baker had a room we could stay in. It was clearly the matrimonial room, accessed via a steep set of wooden stairs, filled with a vast bed. Probably generations of bakers had been conceived, born and most likely died there too. We were treated to an evening meal, and a breakfast the next day. We had long discussions with the baker, and other neighbours who had come to join in after supper, when we all quaffed the local wine – our arrival had obviously become an 'event'.

Apart from the church, there was nothing in the village – the osteria, the baker, and the men at work, along with the older women, all doing heavy agricultural work by hand and donkey. Then cooking and sewing. None of them had ever been to Rome, so traffic was almost unknown, hence the excitement when we arrived in a Topolino with our Roma number plates. There was no television and no cinema; they made their own entertainment – when they had time and weren't too tired. But they were kindness personified; thrilled to hear we'd been on trains – and in aeroplanes! And to London! We saw no other cars at all. No telephones. It would seem there was no one with a camera, and many were a bit scared of having their photo taken. The supermarket had not been invented then. They pretty well grew everything they ate, and probably made much of their bedding and clothes; where the ancient furniture came from originally, I know not. Perhaps families got together to purchase items which would have been delivered by local drivers with pickup trucks that could navigate the rough tracks and narrow streets. And then the menfolk would have carried it all into the houses.

This was nearly seventy years ago, before the autostrade were built, and many places remained remote and inaccessible. They were all so kind and friendly. Oh, and our night's stay with supper and breakfast for two cost £3.

Tessa knew people from her childhood in Italy and when we went to Turin she looked up an old friend. This elderly soul kindly offered us a drink and I was about to accept when Tessa said we'd just had one, thank you; the small fridge had been opened and I saw there was nothing in it but a bun and about a quarter of a litre of milk. With another friend, also in straitened circumstances living north of Milan, we ate cereal most meals and drank water, plain or for a guest, with a slice of lemon.

Tessa lived off a small allowance, which she shared with a cat and all the strays in her area of Rome. It annoyed me intensely that I'd give her some lire, and she then bought fish for the cats and didn't spend it on herself. Of course, if you give money, you must give it freely without strings ... I know! I know! But it still annoys me! So fresh fish would be bought for her splendid, large white Persian feline ... and then more fish on newspaper would be dropped down from her balcony onto the earth below ... where all the cats would come from miles around to help themselves. Miaowing, spitting and hissing; the fish would smell; the neighbours would complain, and – enough! As you can tell, it bothered me. (An understatement!)

The bathroom had a bidet by the loo; one could be having a private visit there and find the large white Persian feline in the bidet beside you, also performing ... which was somewhat disconcerting. Besides, he would gaze up at you, watching with a fixed stare. Does one stare back? Or look away? What is the general rule of polite loo behaviour? Look away, methinks, like the POWs did when visiting the latrines.

He'd sit on the dressing table by the mirror, admiring himself; he leant back once – and fell off backwards. Serve him right, I thought. He was spectacularly large and lovely – and knew it.

On one occasion I said I'd treat Tessa and we went to Austria and Germany and then back into Northern Italy. In the Italian Dolomites, nearing the Brenner Pass, we enquired of rural communities whether they had a zimmer – jah; and can we essen here? Jah – was essen? Huhne? Pointing at a chicken. Jah, we said. Gut, she said, and took a hen and strangled it forthwith. We both blenched, and made our way to our room. It was raining ... and continued to rain most of our four day trip. As the Topolino had a soft top, it began growing moss both inside and out ... which was worrying. We started asking first for a zimmer and then *haben zie ein garage, bitte?* as this became essential.

We'd bought postcards and stamps in Austria, but by mistake drove through it and out into Germany before we'd posted them. Austria seems to be quite narrow ... we were so wet and cold that in one place we spent the evening playing cards on our beds wrapped in those enormous continental duvets they had in those days. And sipping red wine, for internal heating.

Then we came to Strasbourg, and it was sunny and fine, but we could find no cheap rooms; waiters would offer to lend us rooms or take us 'somewhere special', which worried us somewhat so we didn't accept their help. Finally in the biggest, best, most expensive hotel we got a twin bedded on the ground floor. So I said, this is my treat Tessa; we're here, so let's enjoy it. And we did; bisque d'homard; followed by chateaubriand; followed by pavlova? – not sure now. Wine of course, and then ... a stomach ache that forced me to retire to my bed. Tummy bloated, to such a degree I couldn't get out of my dress. Tessa got scissors and unpicked the side seam. I lay there, bloated.

Tessa rang for Fernet Branca – as she said, it works wonders; it's a digestivo and in no time your stomach will subside. It took a while, but eventually the balloon that was my tum, went down. Ever since then, I have treasured Fernet Branca – it tastes horrid, but it works.

That was a memorable visit to Strasbourg; unfortunately we'd run out of money when it came to leaving. I had enough to pay the bill, but nothing left for the row of flunkies waiting for us to walk past and reward them on departure. So I'm ashamed to say, we lifted the window of our bedroom, put our cases out and then climbed out after them; scurried to our car and started the trip back to Rome.

Assisi was a favourite place to drive to. On one visit we discovered a film was being made about St Francis and Santa Chiara ... so there were streets blocked off and film crews everywhere. We drove through the piazza in front of the basilica by mistake which caused a rumpus; they had to stop filming and remove us. That didn't make us popular; later that evening we went to the local cinema and the actors were all there too. But we were charming and everyone chatted in a friendly way – they were probably glad to have met some English speakers. Our heroine, Santa Chiara, was a very blonde, very American, very made-up and red-lipped lass. Hard to visualize her as a nun in a wimple.

Of course there were very few tourists in the fifties and girls certainly didn't travel or go out on their own. Driving back to Rome one evening I had not followed the curve of the road down a winding hill, but gone straight down the centre as there were no cars in sight. Two traffic police stepped out at the bottom and waved me down with their little lollipop baton.

Inspection of documentation followed and I was informed I had broken the law by not keeping to the side of the road as required. I said I thought that with no traffic, it was safe to do as I had. The law is the law, I was solemnly advised. My passenger, another friend from the office, said, "In England we use our common sense", which didn't go down well. You're not in England and we had better inspect your car and see if the mirrors are legal, and the tyres, and the number plates … etc.

This latter was hanging on with a bit of wire I'd added. As we were clearly making enemies and likely to get a bigger fine – and you paid on the spot – I told my friend to be quiet and not say anything. Leave it to me. So I started changing the atmosphere and seeking advice from them. Soon they were asking where we were going, so late in the evening; two girls alone … they knew a good place a few kilometres on and they could come and join us when they were off duty etc …

Really? I said; that is so helpful of you and so kind – and it would be fun to meet up. Yes, we'll see you later. We got away with it that time, luckily. Needless to say, we drove straight on home.

I recall another (Roman) occasion when we were about to be fined on the spot for parking where we shouldn't and my female passenger burst into great sobs and tears and sat on the pavement and wept, looking so upset that the policeman crouched beside her, patting her shoulder and trying to comfort her. He cancelled the fine. It was against the law to embrace, let alone kiss, in public. So young lovers would go to the railway station and pretend they were saying farewell to each other prior to some long, agonising separation. Embraces and stolen kisses, along with close clinches were more likely to be overlooked by the law there.

Not all police or carabinieri were 'nice'. On the tram, squashed up, standing in rush hour one had to fight off hands that were trying to 'have a feel', and a white gloved male hand that I swatted turned out to belong to the carabiniere standing a few feet away. In full uniform too! Men!

Mind you, now I would miss it – the wolf whistles, the admiring looks, the efforts to look up your skirt as you got into a very low (very expensive) sports car! It was a sport – and you tried to beat them at their own game by skilful manoeuvring as you got in and out of vehicles. One felt very feminine and special and attractive. Yes! Even I did! Girls wore skirts, of course, and rode side saddle on their boyfriend's Vespa or Lambretta. So feminine and elegant.

Once my male driver did a rude 'two horns' sign at a Vespa driver who'd cut in front of our car; he turned to grin at us, shake his head and point at his priest's collar! No! He wasn't 'cornuto'! This has almost stopped now, I think. Some years later when with a female friend we were followed and being chatted to (annoyingly), so I said would you mind leaving us alone? If we wanted to be with our boyfriends we would be. And the two lads apologised and left. What a change in behaviour! But I miss it – it was fun, and it made me feel good! That's probably very unPC!

Tessa and I lost touch towards the end of her life; she returning to this country to be near her sisters. I was asked to visit her and see if I could help. But it didn't work out; Tessa had got involved with some religious sect or cult and could talk and think of nothing else. This surprised me as she had been helped a lot by nuns in Italy and I'd thought she would turn to them again when in need. Not so.

But Rome and Tessa were a very enjoyable chapter in my life. She would vet any boyfriend I produced and was always cheerful despite her health problems. Her modern flat on the northern outskirts of Rome had a terrace which overlooked the countryside and there was little or no traffic. The hills were silhouetted in the distance as night fell, the crepuscule slowly spreading across the land. In the spring, the nightingales would begin to sing and the night sky was filled with music.

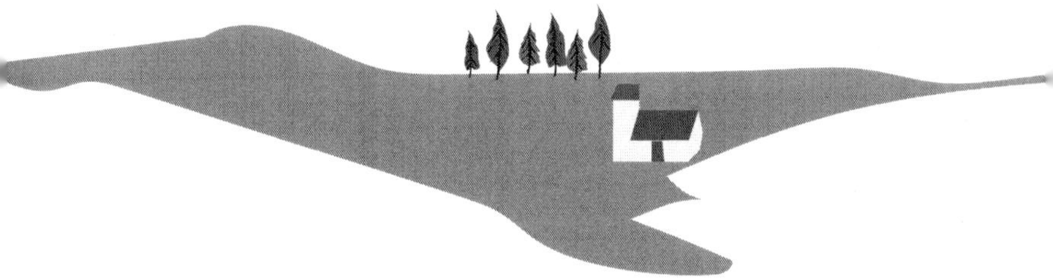

Dragonfly Lane re-visited

I thought I would revisit Dragonfly Lane
Get on my bike and cycle again
Past the overgrown hedges and brambles too high
That cover the fencing and reach for the sky.

They're out of control and, yes, I confess
Much pruning is needed; it's really a mess
With the fencing collapsing and multiple holes
Where rabbits, and foxes, and badgers and voles
All make their way unhindered. There'll come the day
When it's cut back and thinned, old growth cleared away.

That's the lane's west side. But now on its east
The fence is much lower; it sags, but at least
The brambles are trimmed, the willows are small,
A little stream trickles and waters it all –
Here insects and mammals and small birds have got
Good shelter and food in this undisturbed spot.

Thank goodness for that! I did not expect
The big hedge to be missing, and not to detect
Any self-seeded saplings or bushes, no green
At all where those brambles and berries had been.
It was stark, it was bare. The whole hedge was stripped
Away, and dug up, grubbed up; totally ripped
Out. All gone.

Now no willow herb is showing,
No dandelion, mallow or stonecrop growing,
No thistle, or daisy, no cow parsley seed.
No nothing at all: not one windblown weed.

But I cannot complain, it was needed I'm sure.
The previous fence was no longer secure.
So strong concrete posts are lining the lane,
With fresh chain link fencing – it's all new again;
And lovely loose coils of shiny razor wire
Are its crowning glory: what's not to admire!

The Tuscan Palazzo

How lovely the valley, so fertile and green;
Encompassed by hills, with mist in between
The distant mountain ranges.

The rough track wound,
Dusty and white, over the hard, stony ground;
Through fields and small terraces covered in vines,
Fig trees and olives – and those austere lines
That are the Cypress trees' dark beauty.

Wound on until
The old Palazzo stood there, kind against the hill;
Its weathered stone warm-coloured, silent and serene.
At ease with itself, the present – with all that had been.

ACKNOWLEDGEMENTS

This book is dedicated to my family and friends. Special thanks to Lorna Brookes of Crumps Barn Studio for her encouragement and endless patience. My computer efforts must have been a nightmare.

ABOUT THE AUTHOR

Anne Swan's childhood was idyllic, with dogs and ponies, happy schools and holidays abroad. Her work as a secretary both in the UK and overseas was interesting and enjoyable. Later, she was happily married. Anne is also a pianist and composer.

If you loved this book,
please leave a review ...

**The best place to leave a review is on
Waterstones.com or on Amazon**

Reviews make our authors happy and help us to
share news of their work with more readers.
Thank you for your support!

Did you know that this book has been ethically
printed in the UK on FSC certified paper made
from a mixture of fibre from responsibly managed
woodlands and recycled material?

Crumps Barn Studio
crumpsbarnstudio.co.uk

If you loved this book, you'll love these other personal histories ...

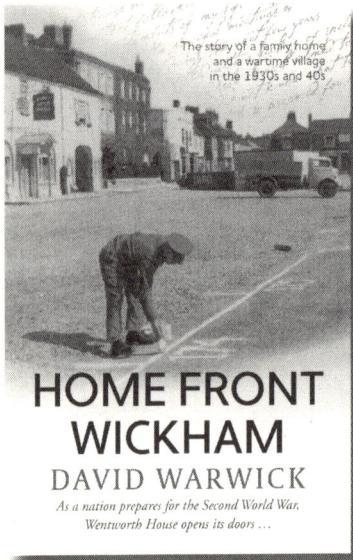

Crumps Barn Studio
beautiful bookshelf reads